THE FANCIEST FLOWER

By Summer Benton

HARPER
An Imprint of HarperCollinsPublishers

HarperCollins Children's Books, a division of HarperCollins Publishers, 195 Broadway, New York, NY 10007

HarperCollins Publishers, Macken House, 39/40 Mayor Street Upper, Dublin 1, D01 C9W8, Ireland

The Fanciest Flower
Copyright © 2026 by Summer Benton
All rights reserved. Manufactured in Capriate San Gervasio, Italy.
No part of this book may be used or reproduced in any manner whatsoever without written permission except in the case of brief quotations embodied in critical articles and reviews. Without limiting the exclusive rights of any author, contributor, or the publisher of this publication, any unauthorized use of this publication to train generative artificial intelligence (AI) technologies is expressly prohibited. HarperCollins also exercises their rights under Article 4(3) of the Digital Single Market Directive 2019/790 and expressly reserves this publication from the text and data mining exception.
harpercollins.com
Library of Congress Control Number: 2024952221
ISBN: 978-0-06-337357-0
The artist used Adobe Photoshop to create the digital illustrations for this book.
Typography by Marisa Rother
25 26 27 28 19 RTLO 10 9 8 7 6 5 4 3 2 1
First Edition

To Mom and Dad

Thanks for the soil, the water, and sun.
I couldn't have blossomed without all your love.

—S.B.

Ferny O'Violet was famous for selling the very best flowers in town. She sold them to babies, bakers, ballerinas—even beagles. Everyone knew they could always find the most beautiful, most sweet-smelling, most flowery flowers at Ferny's.

And she always knew exactly which flower would be perfect for each customer.

But one day, a customer came into Ferny's shop who couldn't find a single flower she liked. She turned up her nose at a rose. She called the lilies silly. "The poppies are sloppy, the lilacs lackluster, and the daffodils make me ill," she sneered.

"I'm having a big party with tons of glamorous guests. And I want a flower for my centerpiece that they've never seen before in their whole fancy lives."

Ferny didn't know what to do, but she couldn't stand to disappoint a customer.

"I might have something in the back," she said.

Ferny frantically rummaged through the cupboard. She searched the spices and snacks. She peeked under pots and pans. She looked behind every bottle and bowl until she found something that might do the trick.

"It's a Fork Flower," Ferny proclaimed. "It may look and feel like an ordinary fork, but in fact, it is widely considered the fanciest flower in the whole entire world."

That night at the party, the Fork Flower was a huge hit. It knocked their fancy socks off! The only thing anyone could talk about was how this shiny new flower made every other flower suddenly seem so . . . ordinary.

By the next day, everyone in town had heard about this exotic new Fork Flower. People lined up around the block to get one of their own.

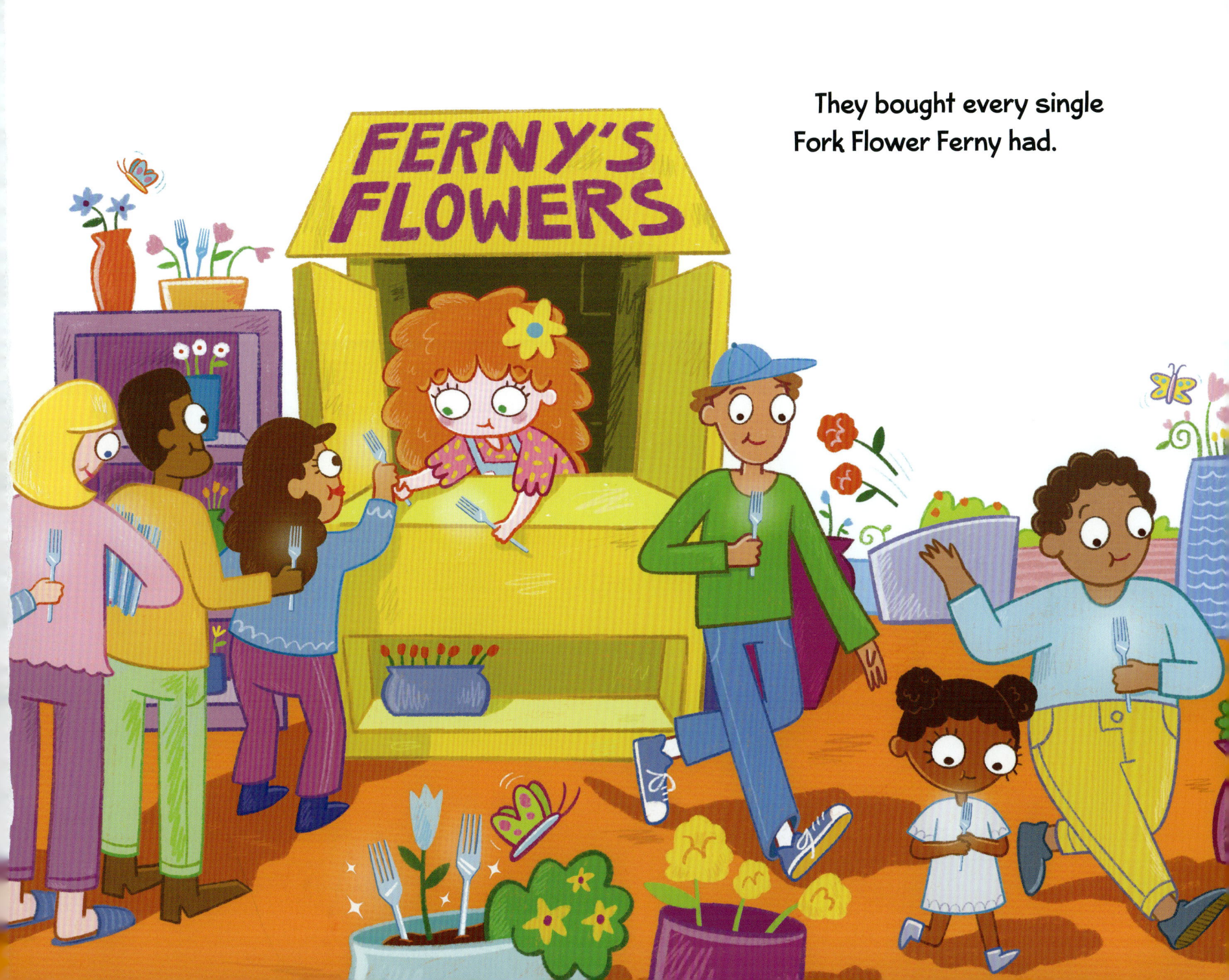

They bought every single Fork Flower Ferny had.

The same thing happened day after day. Ferny was so busy selling forks by the fistful that she didn't have time to care for her real flowers.

As the weeks went by, their stems drooped, their petals fell, and eventually, their sweet flower smell was nowhere to be smelled.

One night, Ferny had just closed her shop when a little boy ran up looking for a flower. Ferny was completely sold out of forks, spoons, knives, and whisks, which she had also sold to the customers as brand-new exotic flowers. But when the boy looked at her with his big hopeful eyes, she knew she couldn't disappoint him.

"I might have something in the back," she said.

Ferny searched everywhere for one more fork for the boy. She combed through the cups and cans. She pulled out the pitchers and plates. She turned over each teacup and tin. She was just about to give up when something caught her eye.

Ferny looked closer and realized it was a flower—a real one!

It had survived all this time on a little puddle of water and a thin ray of sunlight.

Ferny gave the flower to the boy and watched his face light up. As he skipped away, she realized a fork had never made her that happy.

The next day, when the customers arrived at Ferny's shop, they found her waiting with an announcement.

"A Fork Flower is not a flower," she told the crowd. "It's just, you know, a fork."

The customers were shocked.

"I know you guys love them," she said, "and I don't like disappointing you, but I love real flowers, and I miss everything about them. I miss planting them as tiny seeds and watering them every day and singing them their favorite songs."

Suddenly other people started to speak up too.
"Will you grow some more sunflowers?"
"Tulips?"
"Hibiscus?"

Before long, she was happily selling the flowers she loved again.
Ferny hoped she would never see another fork as long as she lived.

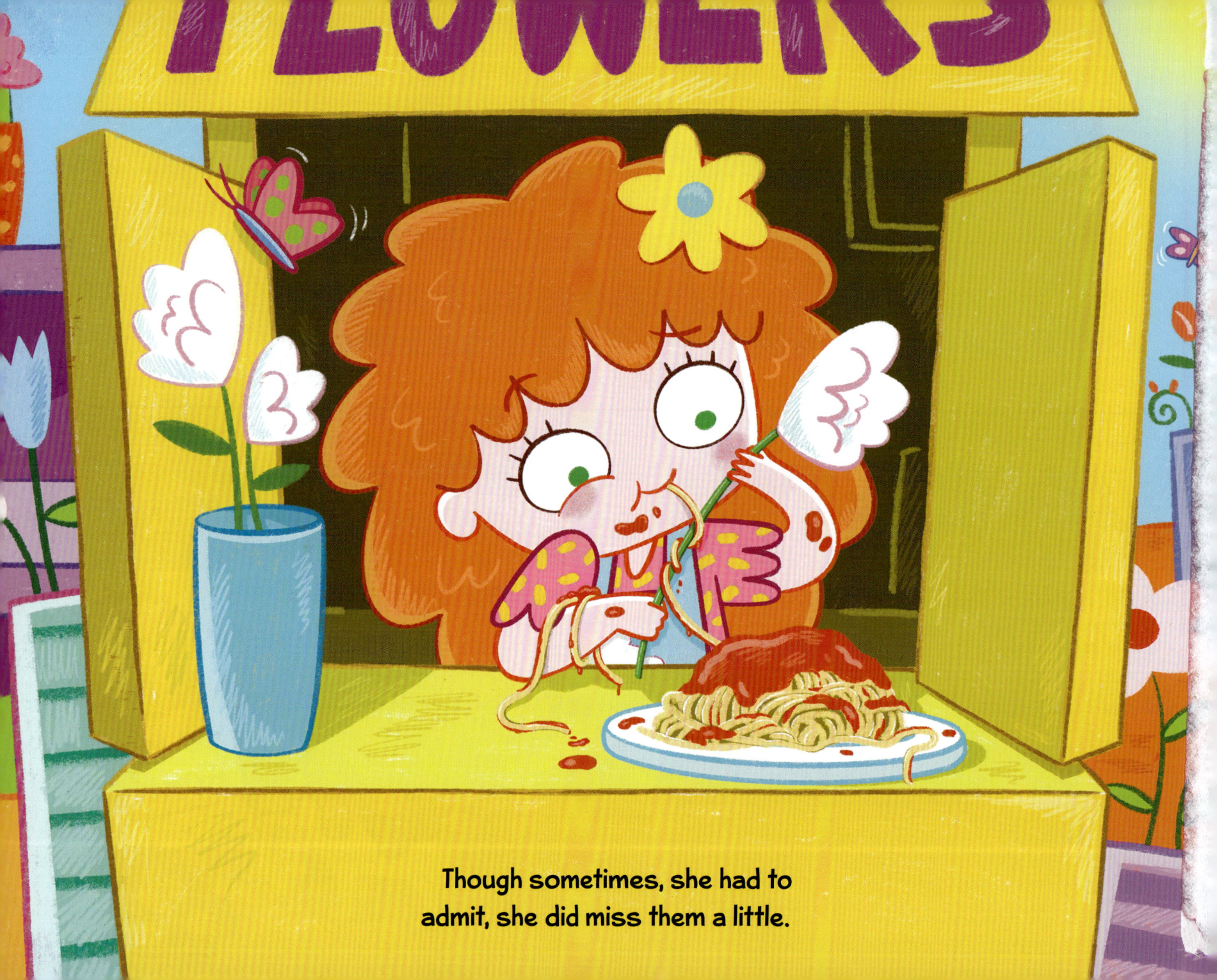
Though sometimes, she had to admit, she did miss them a little.